©1990 Grandreams Limited
This edition published in 1997

Published by
Grandreams Limited
435-437 Edgware Road, Little Venice, London, W2 ITH

Printed in Hong Kong

XM6

CONTENTS

Long ago in a far off country there lived a king who ruled fairly and wisely and seldom took a day off. He always worked very hard and expected his subjects to do the same.

His father, who had ruled before him, had been a lazy king who spent the time enjoying himself. He was always throwing parties and going on holiday and used any excuse to take a day off.

"That pimple on my nose seems to have disappeared," he would say to his wife. "I think I'll declare a national holiday in its honour." And from then on that day would be known as 'Passing of the Pimple Day'.

There was also 'Toenail Trimming Tuesday', 'Dog Bathing Day' and 'Fish Paste Friday', which was a bit like 'Pancake Day'.

There were so many holidays that very little work got done. No crops grew, no houses were built and children hardly ever went to school. The country got poorer and poorer, people went hungry and boys and girls grew up not knowing their ABC.

When the King died, his son came to power and everything changed. He abolished most of the silly holidays introduced by his father; which, at first, wasn't popular with his subjects for they had grown lazy and workshy. But when they saw the new king digging in the fields, sawing wood and hammering in nails, they followed his example and began to work had too.

Gradually the country grew rich again. But, although he could afford to take things easy, the King worked harder than ever.

Cancelled Christmas

"Please turn down the lamps and let us go to sleep," begged the Queen. "It's way past midnight."

The King was sitting up in bed polishing his riding boots.

"And why are you cleaning those? You never go riding."

"No, dear. Riding's a complete waste of time and energy. I've much more important things to do like weeding the flower beds and cutting the lawns." The King gazed around the room. "Would you like me to shine your dancing shoes while I'm at it?"

"What on earth for?" snapped the Queen. "I never go dancing. When was the last time we gave a ball or a party? We don't even celebrate my birthday anymore," she said, sadly.

The King gave a grin. "So that's why you never look any older. Er . . would you mind moving your head so I can polish those bed knobs."

His wife let out a scream of exasperation and threw a pillow at him.

It was Autumn and the Queen was looking forward to Christmas. It was one of the few holidays left. She was discussing all the arrangements with the Chancellor when the King rushed in clutching a calendar. She was immediately filled with dread.

"I've thought how we can fit more working days into the year," he exclaimed, pleased with himself.

"What do we want with more working days?" asked the Queen, "haven't we enough already?"

"No, my dear, there are never enough. Why, there's that order for eight hundred milking stools for the King of Lagunia and six hundred christening spoons for the . . ."

"All right, all right," said the Queen impatiently. "What are you getting rid of this time, 'Pudding Mixing Day', 'Present Wrapping Wednesday' or 'Snowman Sunday'?"

"Christmas Day!" announced the King, proudly.

"Christmas Day!" echoed the Queen, horrified. "But you can't. I'm making plans."

"Exactly," said the King. "If I get rid of Christmas all those other days go too. They won't be necessary." He turned to the Chancellor. "Put out a decree at once that this year Christmas will be cancelled."

"Oh will it?" thought the Queen. "We'll see about that."

His subjects weren't very pleased with the news, but they simply grumbled amongst themselves and hoped the King would change his mind. He didn't.

The night before Christmas Eve, the Queen lay awake waiting for

her husband to fall asleep. Then, as soon as she heard midnight chime, she slipped out of bed and crept round the castle changing the date on all the calendars. Instead of reading December 24th, she had put them forward a day to December 25th - Christmas Day. Then she went back to bed to wait for morning.

"Would you believe it it's Christ . . . er, December 25th already," said the King. "Doesn't time fly?

Well I'd better be off. Got to clear the snow off the castle drawbridge. There weren't any presents, I mean parcels left for me, were there?"

The Queen shook her head and the King left, looking disappointed.

It was lunchtime when they met again, seated either end of the long banqueting table.

"It does look gloomy in here," commented the King. "Don't you think a few decorations might brighten it up a bit?"

"They might," said the Queen, "but with everyone working it hardly seems worth doing. Ah, lunch."

A servant placed before them plates of bread and cheese. The King's face fell. "No turkey? No stuffing? No cranberry sauce?"

"No dear," answered the Queen. "This is an everyday working lunch."

The King spent a cold afternoon breaking the ice on the castle horse troughs. When he came in at tea time he was looking forward to a slice of iced fruit cake, but all he got was bread and dripping.

"I don't suppose there's a mince pie or two lying around," he asked.

"Oh no," the Queen told him. "I only make those at Christmas."

The King looked thoroughly miserable.

"I think I may have made a terrible mistake, cancelling Christmas," he sighed. "I miss the presents, the decorations, the food and the fun. Tomorrow I shall put it back on the calendar. What a pity we'll have to wait a whole year to enjoy it."

The Queen decided that he had learned his lesson and it was time to tell him about the trick she had played. ". . . . . . . and so you see, dear, it's still only Christmas Eve," she explained.

The King gave a whoop of joy and sent out messengers to tell his subjects that tomorrow was a holiday and that they should stop work and prepare for Christmas Day.

And when the Queen's birthday came round, he threw the biggest party that the castle had ever seen.

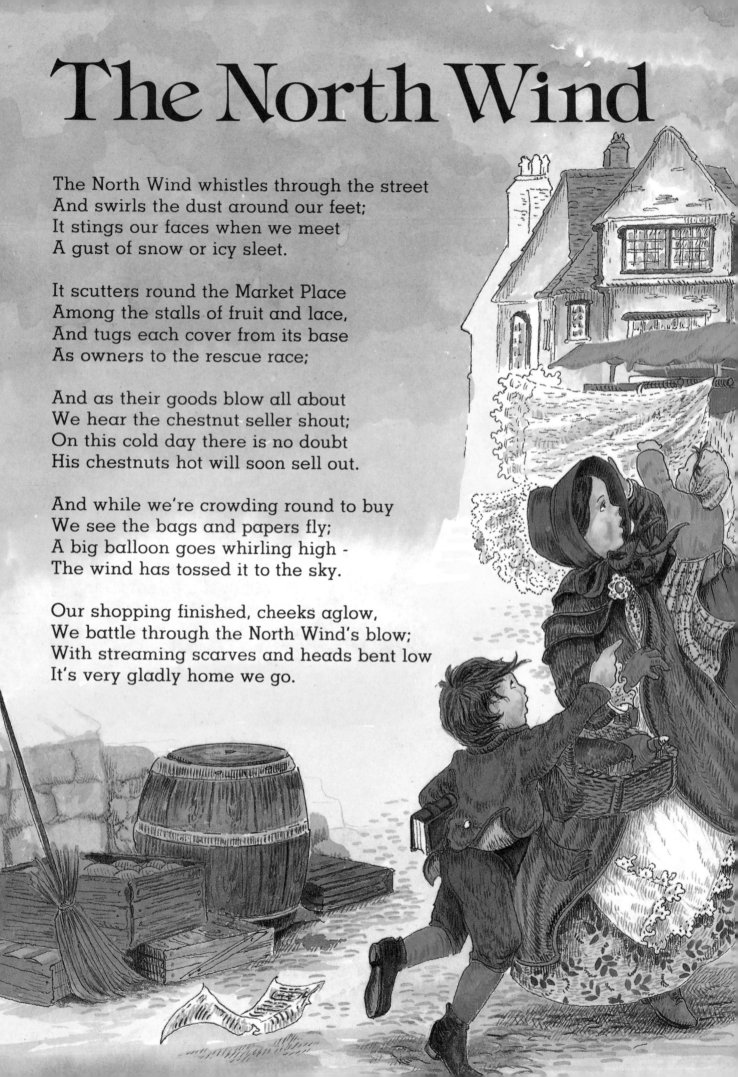

The North Wind

The North Wind whistles through the street
And swirls the dust around our feet;
It stings our faces when we meet
A gust of snow or icy sleet.

It scutters round the Market Place
Among the stalls of fruit and lace,
And tugs each cover from its base
As owners to the rescue race;

And as their goods blow all about
We hear the chestnut seller shout;
On this cold day there is no doubt
His chestnuts hot will soon sell out.

And while we're crowding round to buy
We see the bags and papers fly;
A big balloon goes whirling high -
The wind has tossed it to the sky.

Our shopping finished, cheeks aglow,
We battle through the North Wind's blow;
With streaming scarves and heads bent low
It's very gladly home we go.

A Picture To Paint

If you enjoyed reading the poem, *The North Wind*, then you will love colouring this picture. Use the one on the previous pages as a guide and then with your pencils, paints, crayons or markers carefully colour it in. Then when you have done that see how many objects beginning with `B' you can find in the picture.

THE LITTLE FIR TREE

The little fir tree grew in the middle of a spinney, amongst the great, tall trees. He could hear all the big trees whispering to each other, high above him, and wondered if he would ever be tall enough for the other trees to take any notice of him.

All through the spring and summertime, rabbits and fieldmice tumbled about under the little fir tree's branches. In the autumn, too, the squirrels tickled his roots as they pushed nuts into secret hideaways in the ground, so he was never really lonely.

But as soon as the winter came, all the small creatures tucked themselves safely away in their burrows and nests, and there was no-one to talk to, except the robin.

In the cold weather the robin would fly over to the farmhouse to pick up breadcrumbs that John and Judith threw out. They lived in the farmhouse which the little fir tree could just see, on the far side of the valley.

The robin often looked through the windows and when he flew back to the spinney he would tell the little fir tree what John and Judith were doing.

One day in December, the robin flew back to the spinney in great excitement. "What *do* you think?" he asked, hopping up and down. "Something *very* strange is happening in the farmhouse. John and Judith have been making long chains out of pretty paper. Red, yellow, blue and green, all sorts of colours. Then they hung them all over the room.

"After that, they went into the garden and picked a lot of holly and some branches of mistletoe that grow on the old apple tree in the orchard.

"*Then* Judith said: 'Shall we go over to the spinney now?' I expect they'll be here in a minute. I wonder what they are going to do next?"

The little fir tree quivered with excitement. John and Judith hadn't been to the spinney since the summer, when they had picnics on sunny days.

But now it was far too cold for a picnic. Snow lay on the ground, the north wind was blowing and the robin had to fluff out his feathers to keep warm. "Oh, I can see them

coming now!" he chirped.

John and Judith, dressed in warm scarves and woolly gloves were tramping across the snow. John carried a spade over his shoulder and Judith was pulling a sledge.

"What do you think they are going to do?" whispered the little fir tree.

"I've no idea," chirped the robin. "I'll fly over to the hedge and watch."

John and Judith came into the spinney, all out of breath. "That was a long walk," gasped Judith. "Now, where is that little fir tree?"

The little fir tree rustled his branches in surprise. John looked round. "Here it is. I remember

seeing it here last summer."

To the little fir tree's surprise, John began to carefully dig the ground all round him. Then the spade went under his roots and he was lifted up, out of the ground. It felt very strange.

John and Judith put the little fir tree on the sledge and began to pull it back to the farmhouse. The robin followed just behind. "Hold on tightly," he chirped.

When they reached the house, the little fir tree was lifted from the sledge and planted in a wooden tub. Then he was carried indoors. "Where shall we put it?" asked John.

"By the window," said Judith. "So that everyone coming along the

road can see it."

Carefully they put the tub down by the window and the little fir tree peeped outside. The robin was waiting on the windowsill. "What a funny thing to happen," whispered the fir tree. "I wonder what they are going to do now?"

Judith had opened a big bag and inside were all kinds of glittering decorations. "Here's the star to go on the very top branch," she cried.

"And here are the fairy lights," said John.

They began to cover the little fir tree with tinsel and brightly coloured balls until he was shining and sparkling all over. They then switched on the fairy lights.

"Oh, look at it now," breathed Judith. "It's the loveliest Christmas tree we've ever had."

When John and Judith had gone out of the room the robin tapped on the window with his beak. "What ever has happened to you?" he asked.

"Did you hear what they said?" whispered the fir tree. "They called me a *Christmas tree*."

"How strange, " said the robin, "but you do look very grand." He hopped along the windowsill to take a better look, then he said: "I'm off now to sleep in the warm barn tonight. I'll see you in the morning."

John and Judith had gone to bed early, so the little fir tree stood watching the fire burning lower in the hearth. It was nearly midnight when he heard a jingling noise in the distance.

He looked out of the window and by the light of the moon he could see a sledge, pulled by a team of reindeer. The sledge stopped by the farmhouse and out stepped Santa Claus.

Santa picked up a big sack of toys from the sledge and then he suddenly saw the little Christmas tree, shining through the window. "Hello," he chuckled. "My, you're the grandest little Christmas tree I've seen tonight.

"I always give a special present to the best Christmas tree I find," said Santa. "Now what would you like most of all?"

The little fir tree rustled shyly. "Oh, most of all I would like to grow into a big tree quickly."

"I think I have just the present for you," Santa told him, dipping his hand into the sack and pulling out a small bottle, tied with a ribbon. "If this mixture is put round your roots when you are planted in the ground again, you will quickly grow into a tall tree."

"Oh, thank you," replied the little fir tree, "and have you a present for my friend, the robin?"

"Yes," said Santa. "I've got something that the robin will like very much." He opened the window and tied the bottle and a present for the robin onto the fir tree's branches.

"Now I must take some presents to John and Judith," he said. "Goodbye, little Christmas tree."

The next morning, the robin flew down to the windowsill and tapped on the window. "Merry Christmas," he chirped. "Is breakfast ready yet?"

"Merry Christmas," replied the little fir tree. "Santa Claus left a present for you."

The window had been left open a little way, so the robin hopped through and began to peck open his present. "Look," he chirped, as pleased as he could be. "It's a packet of my favourite birdseed."

He hopped back out of the window with his present in his beak, just as John and Judith came running into the room with their new toys.

The little fir tree glittered and shone all the Christmastime. Later on, when John and Judith took him back to the spinney and planted him in the ground, they found a small bottle of special mixture, though they had no idea who had put it there.

They read the label, and poured the mixture round his roots. Then the little fir tree grew and grew, until he was the tallest tree for miles around.

Snow For Christmas

Tony and Carol had been to the village shop to buy some Christmas decorations. Now they were on their way home along Holly Lane. Carol kept stopping to peep at the paper chains and the tinsel for the Christmas tree which were in the bag she was carrying. "Come along," called Tony. "You can look at them properly when we get home."

"Do let's blow up one of the balloons now," begged Carol.

"Oh, all right," agreed Tony. He pulled out a big yellow one and began to puff hard into it. Then he found a piece of string in his pocket to tie round it.

"Isn't it a super one?" cried Carol.

"Oh, my," said a voice above them. "That's a lovely big moon you've got!" They looked up, and there was an elf sitting on a branch of a tree.

"It's not a moon, it's a balloon," explained Tony, and he threw the balloon up in the air so that the elf could look at it.

"Well, it looks like a moon," replied the elf. "I'll swap you a wish for it."

"Shall we?" Tony asked Carol.

"Yes," Carol replied. "It would be exciting to wish for something very special."

"Done!" said the elf. "Now what would you like to wish for?"

"I know what I'd like," said Carol. "Could you make it snow for Christmas?"

"Yes," the elf told her. "But we shall have to go up to Cloudland and see the snow fairies. Close your eyes and wish."

So Tony and Carol closed their eyes tightly and wished hard. Then they could feel the wind lifting them up and up.

"Very easily," replied the snow fairies. So they opened the gates of Cloudland and pushed the snowclouds across the sky.

"Come along," said the elf. "We'll go back to the wood now." Tony and Carol closed their eyes tightly and the wind took them down and down until they were back in Holly Lane.

"The snowflakes are beginning to fall already," cried the elf. "I'm going to show my friends my special moon. Goodbye!" And off he ran with the yellow balloon bobbing behind him.

Tony and Carol waved goodbye and then hurried all the way back home through the snow, to put up their decorations ready for Christmas.

Prince Perkin's Problem Pet

Prince Perkin lived in a large castle with his father, the King, and his mother, the Queen. But they were always so busy ruling the country that Perkin spent most of his time with his pets.

He already had a pony, a dog, a cat, a rabbit and a hamster. Not to mention the goldfish in the royal fountain and doves that would eat out of his hand. But he loved animals and was always looking for new pets to add to his collection.

One day the royal woodcutter came to the castle with an odd-looking animal. "What is it?" asked Perkin, looking at the tiny creature, which was

about the size of a kitten. It had wings, a spiked tail and green scales all over its body.

"It's a baby dragon," said the woodcutter. "I found it wandering about on the far side of the forest. It's too young to be left all by itself."

"What shall we give it to eat?" asked Perkin.

"I don't think dragons are too fussy about their food," said the woodcutter. So Perkin offered it a bun and some chocolate, and the baby dragon gobbled them up, blowing out little puffs of smoke as though it really enjoyed the snack.

"I'll call him Puffer," decided Perkin.

The King and Queen were not too sure about Prince Perkin's new pet. "You can keep him for a bit and see how well he behaves," the King told Perkin. "But don't let him get in anyone's way."

Puffer soon learnt to beg for his food and he would sit, and lie down quietly when ordered. He even got quite clever at catching tennis balls in his mouth and would bring them straight back to Perkin - though they were sometimes a bit scorched by his hot breath.

There was only one real problem. As the weeks went by, Puffer grew bigger and bigger. He grew as big as a large dog, then he reached the size of a pony. "He will soon be as large as an elephant," complained the Queen. "Something will have to be done about him."

"It's time that dragon went back to the wild," the King told Prince Perkin. "You can't keep him for ever and he must be big enough to look after himself now. Besides, he may get dangerous. You never know with dragons."

Perkin pleaded to be allowed to keep his pet and Puffer even tried to lick the King's face, which didn't really help. The King very firmly told the woodcutter to take the dragon back to the place where it had been found.

So the woodcutter put Puffer on a lead and took him away to the far side of the forest. There he let the dragon off the lead and hurried away so the dragon couldn't follow him.

Puffer played quite happily for a while, running through the long grass and chasing butterflies amongst the flowers. But then he felt a little bit

hungry and decided it was time to go back home. But he couldn't find the right path. He began to run round in circles, opening his wings and flapping them as he tried to remember which way he had been brought through the forest. Then he felt his wings lifting him into the air and he discovered, for the first time, that he could *fly*.

Puffer flew right over the treetops and in next to no time he was back at the castle. He was surprised to see the drawbridge had been pulled up, but he landed close to it and began scratching to be let in.

The drawbridge had been raised because the King's soldiers had seen
an enemy army marching towards the castle. Then Puffer heard a noise
behind him and turning round, he saw the enemy soldiers getting ready to
fire their big cannon.

BOOM! BOOM! BOOM! They fired the big guns and the cannonballs
came whizzing towards the castle. Puffer opened his mouth and caught
them all, just like tennis balls.

Then he flew towards the enemy soldiers, carrying the cannonballs
back, so that they could fire them again. He thought this game was going
to be great fun. But when the soldiers saw a dragon flying towards them,

they left the big guns and ran away as fast as their legs would carry them.

Puffer was disappointed because nobody wanted to play with him and he walked back to the castle with his tail between his legs. But then Prince Perkin and all the King's soldiers came rushing out to meet him, cheering.

"You've beaten the whole enemy army, so you must stay and guard the castle," cried Perkin, patting Puffer's scaly nose.

"Quite right," said the Queen. "After all, he must be fully grown by now and he's very well trained."

They all made such a fuss of Puffer that the King never again dared to suggest that Prince Perkin's pet dragon should be sent back to the wild.

The Twelve Days Of Christmas

The first day of Christmas
My true love sent to me
A partridge in a pear tree.

The second day of Christmas
My true love sent to me
Two turtle doves, and
A partridge in a pear tree.

The third day of Christmas
My true love sent to me
Three French hens,
Two turtle doves, and
A partridge in a pear tree.

The fourth day of Christmas
My true love sent to me
Four colly birds,
Three French hens,
Two turtle doves, and
A partridge in a pear tree.

The fifth day of Christmas
My true love sent to me
Five gold rings,
Four colly birds,
Three French hens,
Two turtle doves, and
A partridge in a pear tree.

The sixth day of Christmas
My true love sent to me
Six geese a-laying,
Five gold rings,
Four colly birds,
Three French hens,
Two turtle doves, and
A partridge in a pear tree.

The seventh day of Christmas
My true love sent to me
Seven swans a-swimming,
Six geese a-laying,
Five gold rings,
Four colly birds,
Three French hens,
Two turtle doves, and
A partridge in a pear tree.

The eighth day of Christmas
My true love sent to me
Eight maids a-milking,
Seven swans a-swimming,
Six geese a-laying,
Five gold rings,
Four colly birds,
Three French hens,
Two turtle doves, and
A partridge in a pear tree.

The ninth day of Christmas
My true love sent to me
Nine drummers drumming,
Eight maids a-milking,
Seven swans a-swimming,
Six geese a-laying,
Five gold rings,
Four colly birds,
Three French hens,
Two turtle doves, and
A partridge in a pear tree.

The tenth day of Christmas
My true love sent to me
Ten pipers piping,
Nine drummers drumming,
Eight maids a-milking,
Seven swans a-swimming,
Six geese a-laying,
Five gold rings,
Four colly birds,
Three French hens
Two turtle doves, and
A partridge in a pear tree.

The eleventh day of Christmas
My true love sent to me
Eleven ladies dancing,
Ten pipers piping,
Nine drummers drumming,
Eight maids a-milking,
Seven swans a-swimming,
Six geese a-laying,
Five gold rings,
Four colly birds,
Three French hens,
Two turtle doves, and
A partridge in a pear tree.

The twelfth day of Christmas
My true love sent to me
Twelve lords a-leaping,
Eleven ladies dancing,
Ten pipers piping,
Nine drummers drumming,
Eight maids a-milking,
Seven swans a-swimming,
Six geese a-laying,
Five gold rings,
Four colly birds,
Three French hens,
Two turtle doves, and........

A partridge in a pear tree.

The Goat That Ate The Rainbow

There was once a greedy white goat that ate anything he could find. He ate the grass in his field and the thistles round the edge, and any bit of green hedge he could reach.

One day he chewed his way right through the hedge and got into the farmer's garden. Then he ate all the washing the farmer's wife had put out on the line to dry.

"That goat is more trouble than all the other animals on the farm," grumbled the farmer's wife.

"We'll give him one more chance to change his ways," said the farmer, as he mended the gap in the hedge.

But one morning the greedy goat had swallowed every bit of grass he could find in his field and was looking round for something else to eat. Suddenly it began to rain, so he ran into his little shed at the end of the field to take shelter.

The rain beat down on the tin roof, the lightning flashed and the thunder rolled. The greedy goat didn't like it at all. "I hope it stops soon because I'm feeling *hungry*," he bleated.

At last everything went quite. When the goat looked out of his shed he saw that the rain had stopped and a big rainbow was in the sky. The end of the rainbow reached right down into the goat's field. "I wonder if it's good to eat?" he said to himself. He trotted out of his shed and began nibbling at the end of the rainbow.

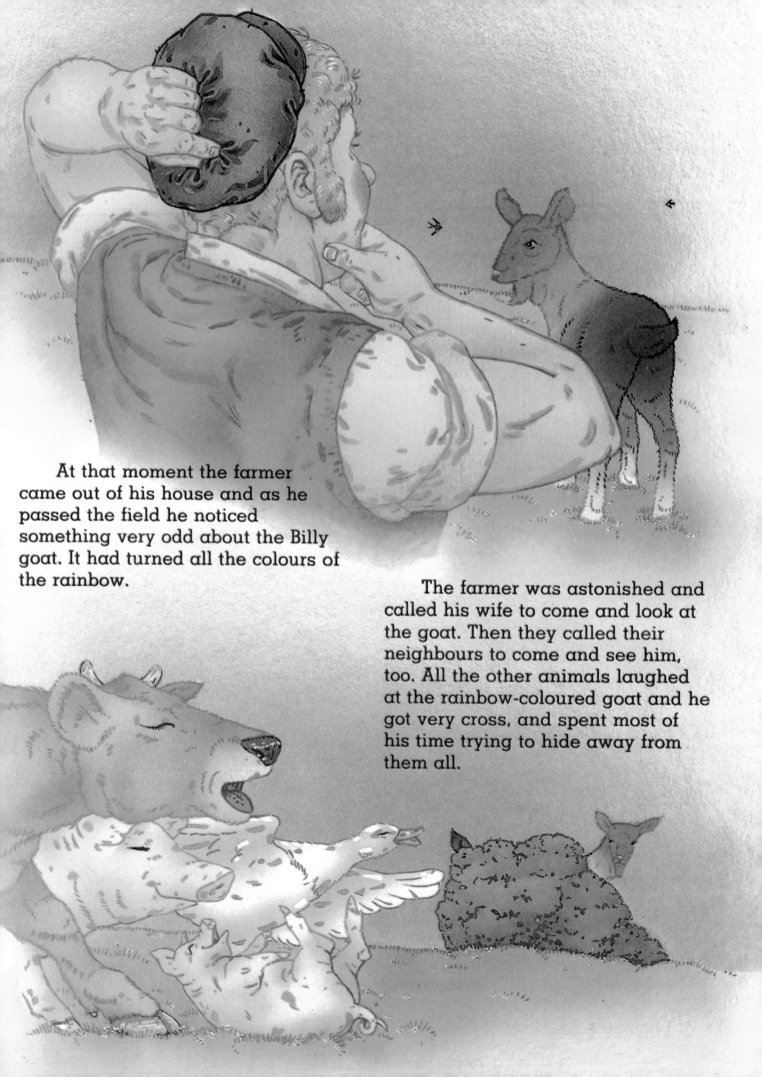

At that moment the farmer came out of his house and as he passed the field he noticed something very odd about the Billy goat. It had turned all the colours of the rainbow.

The farmer was astonished and called his wife to come and look at the goat. Then they called their neighbours to come and see him, too. All the other animals laughed at the rainbow-coloured goat and he got very cross, and spent most of his time trying to hide away from them all.

While the goat was hiding he couldn't reach his food, so he ate less and less as the days went by. Then his coat began to moult, and each day the farmer's wife combed out the long, silky hairs and made them into thread on her spinning wheel. With the thread she knitted all kinds of pretty coloured clothes to replace the ones the goat had eaten.

The farmer's wife was very pleased with her new clothes, which were all the colours of the rainbow. Then the goat began to grow a new, white coat and the other animals stopped laughing at him.

But after that, the Billy was always very careful about anything he ate, and he was never greedy again.

The Nativity Play

"Please, Miss! Joseph's supposed to come with me, not the three Wise Men," complained the Virgin Mary.

"Yes, Cathy, I know," said the teacher wearily. But you musn't stop every time some little thing goes wrong. Haven't you heard the saying 'the show must go on'?"

From the blank look on Cathy's face it was evident that she hadn't.

"It means," Mrs Peel went on, "that whatever happens don't stop, keep going if the scenery falls down, or your costume falls down or the actor falls down. Now, let's start again, and please try to get it right."

Mrs Peel nodded to the piano and for the umpteenth time that afternoon Mrs Graham played the opening bars to 'Once In Royal David's City'.

Inglenook Infants were rehearsing their nativity play. The school was famous for it. It was put on every year, all the parents came to see it and it usually went very well, but this year nothing seemed to be going right.

Mrs Peel had never done the nativity before. It had always been left to Mrs Morris to organise, but she had retired that summer and the headmistress had asked Mrs Peel to take on the task. "I'm sure you'll make a wonderful job of it," the head had said.

Mrs Peel had thought so too at the time, but now she wasn't so sure. Joseph couldn't remember where he was supposed to stand, the Wise Men kept fidgeting and the Shepherds giggled all the time.

The school bell rang out; it was going home time.

"Please, Miss. Can my auntie come and see the play as well as my mum and dad?" asked Pearl Wilson.

"I expect so," sighed Mrs Peel, although she couldn't imagine why Pearl's auntie or anyone would want to sit through this shambles of a Christmas story.

The next morning there was more rehearsing; this time in costume and on the stage in the big hall.

Someone's mum who kept horses had provided bales of straw to dot about the stage. Mr. Green, the school caretaker, had built a stable and a manger and hung up a large star which, when it worked, lit up. It all looked marvellous and Mrs Peel hoped that once the children put on costumes and got amongst the scenery that it would all come right.

Once again the piano struck up with 'Once In Royal David's City. . .' and Joseph stepped on the hem of Mary's robe so she couldn't move.

"Please, Miss!"

"Keep going, Cathy, keep going," Mrs Peel urged.

This time everyone got onto the stage, but the Wise Men kept staring into the hall forgetting to sing and one of the Shepherds was making rude noises to make others laugh.

"Sam Stevens, stop giggling," she called, trying not to lose her patience. "And hold your lamb the right way round."

That made him giggle all the more.

They hadn't even managed a complete run through when the dinner bell sounded. The performance was to be that afternoon.

Those in the play were allowed to stay in costume and eat a packed lunch up on the stage while the other infants had their dinners on the long tables down on the hall floor. It made the cast feel really important.

Alan, one of the Wise Men, started to show off while 'Miss' wasn't looking. He threw a piece of cheese and pickle sandwich at a Shepherd but it missed and fell into the manger where it had stayed.

After lunch, the tables were cleared away and the benches were turned to face the stage. It wasn't long before parents started to arrive and take their seats for the show.

In a nearby classroom the cast waited for their cue to begin.

"Now, please, dears, sing your words clearly, try not to step on each other's clothes and don't gaze around the room," Mrs Peel told them. "It's the baby Jesus you should be looking at not someone's auntie in the front row." The children giggled, nervously.

"Good luck," she added, as the familiar strains of 'Once In Royal David's City' rang out.

Singing sweetly, they filed onto the stage. First Joseph and then Mary, who laid the baby Jesus in the manger. As she did so she gave a small gasp and Mrs Peel, who was watching from the side of the stage, thought that something had gone wrong and that Cathy was going to stop. But, to her great relief, Cathy did as she'd been told and kept singing and staring wide-eyed into the manger.

As Joseph, the Wise Men and the Shepherds gathered round, they too could see what had made Cathy gasp. It was a little brown mouse sitting in the straw, nibbling a piece of cheese and pickle sandwich which Alan had thrown at lunchtime. It didn't seem the least bit worried about the singing or the presence of a large china doll.

With eyes glued to the munching mouse, the children sang their way through 'The Holly and The Ivy', 'The First Noel' and 'O Come All Ye Faithful', which everyone joined in.

Mrs Peel was delighted. They looked a picture grouped round the manger gazing down at the baby Jesus. It was really quite moving. One or two of the mums were having to dab their eyes with handkerchiefs.

When it was over the children dashed back on stage to look in the manger, but the mouse had gone.

"So that's why none of you could take your eyes off the manger," said Mrs Peel, after Cathy had told her about the mouse.

"It must have come out of one of those bales of straw," said one of the boys, pointing.

Mrs Peel shivered. "Well I hope it's gone back there." She wasn't too keen on mice.

The headmistress tapped her on the shoulder. "Well done, Mrs Peel. A perfectly splendid nativity." Then she lowered her voice. "This year's infants can be a bit of a handful at times. But there they were today, standing round the manger looking just like little angels. I don't know how you did it!"

And Mrs Peel wasn't about to tell her that the success of that year's nativity was entirely due to a little brown mouse and a piece of cheese and pickle sandwich.

The Gnomes' Moon Rocket

Huffy the gnome was just shaking his big yellow duster out of the window when he saw a crowd of other gnomes along the road. "I must see where they are going," said Huffy, who never wanted to miss any fun.

He hurried out of his house, still holding his yellow duster. "What's happening?" he puffed, as he caught up with the others.

"We're going to fly to the moon," shouted the gnomes, who were all very excited.

In a few minutes they came to a field where a big rocketship was standing. The pilot gave Huffy a spacesuit and told him to climb the ladder into the rocketship.

When everyone was ready, the pilot closed the hatch and started the countdown. "Five, four, three, two, one - zero!" he called, and suddenly they zoomed into the air, going higher and higher into the sky.

"We shan't be long now," said the pilot, as he pointed the rocketship towards the moon, far in the distance.

Then the engine began making some very odd banging noises. "Will it be all right?" asked Huffy.

"I hope so," said the pilot. But the engine gave an extra loud bang and the rocketship stopped moving.

"It's broken down, and I'm not much good at repairing engines," admitted the pilot.

Huffy looked out of the window. "This is a fine place to stop," he grumbled. "We're in the middle of nowhere."

"What ever shall we do?" cried all the other gnomes.

Huffy stepped out of the rocketship and floated round to the engine. "Perhaps there's a bit of grit in it," he said to himself. But though he checked the engine, the steering jets and the fuel tanks, he couldn't see anything wrong with them. So he felt in the pocket of his spacesuit for his big yellow duster, so that he could wipe his oily hands on it.

Now Huffy's duster was a magic one that he had bought at the Gnometown Stores only that morning. It was a very special offer, and was supposed to do all the dusting in a twinkling. But in outer space, the magic had a very odd effect.

As Huffy shook out the duster, it began to grow bigger. He shook it again until it grew huge. Then he had an idea.

He tied the duster on the front of the rocketship, like a big sail. Then he told all the other gnomes to

sit on top of the rocket and take a
deep breath. "Now take off your
space helmets and blow hard into
the duster," he ordered.

The gnomes blew and blew,
until the big duster sail billowed out
and the rocketship started moving.
Slowly they sailed through the sky
until they were close to the moon.

Luckily the moon midgets had
seen them coming and their leader
waved to Huffy. "Catch!" he shouted,
and threw out a moonbeam. Huffy
caught the end of the moonbeam
and tied it to the rocketship. Then
all the moon midgets pulled on the
other end, until the rocket went
BUMP! against the side of the moon.

"Welcome to Moonland," said
the moon midget leader. "We have
have aa ... achoo! all been watching
you through our aa ... achoo!
telescope."

"Have you got a cold?" asked
Huffy.

"No. It's the moondust that
makes us sneeze," said the moon
midget. "We keep sweeping it up all
the time, but it's very hard to keep
the moon clean and shining."

The other midgets picked up
their moon brooms and began to
sweep the dust away. Soon Huffy
and all the other gnomes were
sneezing, too.

"I have aa ... achoo! an idea,"
said Huffy. Help me take the duster
sail off the rocketship."

So they took down the sail and spread the huge magic duster on the moon. Huffy borrowed a pair of scissors and cut the big duster into small pieces, and gave a piece to each moon midget.

The moon midgets set to work, polishing the moon with their dusters and soon it was shining very brightly.

"That's simply splendid," cried the moon midget leader. "Now we will help you repair your rocketship."

They discovered the cause of the trouble when they pulled a bit of space-rock out of the engine with a moon magnet. Very soon they had the rocketship ready to take off again.

The moon midgets gave each of the gnomes a packet of moon cheese and crisps, in case they felt hungry on the way home. Then Huffy and the pilot, and the other gnomes, all climbed back into the rocketship.

"Goodbye," called the moon midgets. Come and see us again, one day."

The rocketship shot across the sky and it was not long before it landed safely in Gnometown again.

As the gnomes climbed out, they saw it was already night time. "Look!" Huffy pointed to the sky. "The moon is shining brighter than ever. The moon midgets must be busy with their magic dusters again."

Jimmy and The New Year

It was New Year's Eve and Jimmy and his friends were sledging on Hawthorn Common. Jimmy had a special sledge he'd been given for Christmas, and it went much faster than any of the others.

"Whee!" he shouted as he whizzed down the hill, leaving everyone else far behind. He skidded past a big hawthorn bush and landed in the middle of a soft snowdrift.

"That looks fun. Can I have a ride on your sledge?" asked a small, piping voice. Jimmy sat up in surprise as a little figure in a long white robe crawled out from the bush.

"What are you doing there?" cried Jimmy.

"Hiding from Father Time," came the reply. "I'm the New Year and I'm supposed to start work at midnight. But I want to have a bit of fun first."

"Alright," agreed Jimmy. "Help me pull the sledge to the top of the next hill, then we'll slide down the other side."

When they reached the top, the New Year sat on the sledge behind Jimmy. "Hold tight," cried Jimmy, as the sledge gathered speed.

"This is *tre-men-dous!*" squeaked the New Year, gasping for breath as they shot to the bottom of the steep slope. Then he gave a squeal and pointed to someone in the distance. "It's Father Time!"

Coming towards them was an old man with a long beard. He was leaning on a stick and carried an hour-glass in his hand. "If he catches me I'll get a spanking for running away," said the New Year. "I'm off!" and in a moment he had disappeared.

Father Time came trudging through the snow and sat down on a fallen log. "I'll never catch the New Year," he sighed. "He's such a little rascal. He's got to ring the bells in Time Tower at midnight, to let everyone know the new year has begun."

"The New Year ran away because he was afraid he'd get a spanking if you caught him," explained Jimmy. "But if you'll

promise to forgive him, I'll try to find him for you."

"Oh, very well," agreed Father Time. "But remember, he's got to be at Time Tower before midnight. Now I'll put a bit of magic on your sledge, so that it will slide up hills as well as down them."

So Father Time waved his hourglass over the sledge and Jimmy set off to find the New Year.

Very soon he found a trail of small footprints in the deep snow and he followed them up and down the hills on his sledge. "This is great," chuckled Jimmy, as he sped towards the far edge of the Common. "But I hope I can catch up with that little rascal before it gets too late."

Then he heard a cry for help and there on the edge of the Common was the New Year, stuck fast in a barbed wire fence. "I was trying to get through, but my robe caught on the wire and I can't get free," he wailed.

"I'll help you," said Jimmy. "But first you promise to go to Time Tower."

"But Father Time will be cross with me," cried the New Year.

"He told me he'll forgive you if you come straight back with me," said Jimmy.

"Oh, alright, I promise," replied the New Year, sulkily. "But I'll have to ring the New Year Bells, and that's jolly hard work."

Jimmy untangled the New Year from the barbed wire and they both went back to the sledge. This time the New Year sat in front to guide it.

They slid up and down the hills at a great speed and the New Year enjoyed himself so much he was in a much better mood when Time Tower came in sight.

It was a very tall building and at the top, just below the roof, Jimmy could see three big bells.

Down below, Father Time was waiting for them and he was so pleased to see the New Year, he forgot all about being cross with him. "I'll leave the magic on your sledge so that you can get home quickly," he told Jimmy.

So Jimmy raced away over the snow and by the time he reached home, the moon was shining brightly.

He was allowed to stay up late that night, so he stood by the window and listened carefully for the sound of the New Year Bells. At last they rang out in the distance, DING, DANG, DONG. DING, DANG, DONG!

"Happy New Year!" cried Jimmy's Uncle Mac, coming through the door with a lucky lump of coal and a bunch of balloons. Jimmy chuckled and chose one balloon for himself and one for the New Year, just in case he should see him again on Hawthorn Common.

Duckling Island

Dippy Duckling looked out of the duckpen in the farmyard and saw Mother Duck leading all his brothers and sisters through the gate that led to the duck pond.

"Wait for me!" he quacked, and waddled after them as fast as his little yellow webbed feet would carry him.

Farmer Brown was just going to shut the gate when Dippy came along. "Hurry, Dippy, you're all behind again," he chuckled.

Dippy stuck his beak in the air. "I'm going to be in front of everyone else very soon, you'll see!" he quacked. He rushed off towards the duck pond where all the other ducklings were lined up along the edge.

Mother Duck was already telling them: "I'm going to give you your first swimming lesson. Watch me closely." But Dippy didn't watch. He was waddling so fast, he couldn't stop in time and he fell, *splash!* into the water.

How the other ducklings laughed. "You're in too much of a hurry," called Mother Duck.

But Dippy wasn't listening. He was too busy learning to swim. "Whoops, here I go," he quacked. "This is easy and it's much faster than waddling."

"Don't go too far," called his mother.

"Why not?" asked Dippy.

"Because it's not safe," said Mother Duck.

"Pooh!" answered Dippy. "I'll show everyone that I'm not afraid," and he put his beak in the air and started swimming round the pond.

He looked all around and then began poking his beak into the reeds which grew at the edge of the water. There was a rustling noise and suddenly a frog jumped out of the reeds, right over Dippy's head and landed on a lily pad.

"Be careful what you're doing, young duckling," said the frog, rather crossly. "You woke me up when I was having a quiet nap."

"I was just taking a look at everything," replied Dippy. "The pond is such

a big world to see."

"Pooh! The river is *much* bigger," said the frog.

"The river?" asked Dippy. "What's that like?"

"It's wet, like the pond," the frog told him. "Only the pond always stays still and the river is always going somewhere."

"I'd like to see the river," said Dippy. "Where is it?"

"I'm not telling you," said the frog. "The river's not safe for a small duckling. Stay in the pond until you are bigger."

"I'll find the river by myself," said Dippy, and he put his beak in the air and swam off.

When he got to the other side of the pond he found the water running into a small brook. "Perhaps this is the river," said Dippy. He swam along, looking all round him, and he could feel the water pulling him along, faster and faster.

"Go back, duckling," warned a voice.

At first Dippy didn't know where the voice came from. Then he saw two bright eyes watching him from a hole in the bank. A head popped out and a water rat came down to the water's edge.

"Is this the river?" asked Dippy.

"No, it's only the brook," said the water rat. "The river's not safe for a

small duckling. You'd better go back home."

But Dippy was already being carried away by the water. Faster and faster he went until he could see the big, wide river stretching before him. "I think I'll go back now I've seen the river," said Dippy, and he tried to run round and swim back the way he had come.

But no matter how hard he paddled, he just couldn't swim back to the brook and suddenly the water carried him right into the middle of the river. "Help!" he cried. "What shall I do?"

Then he saw an island just in front of him. He swam as close as he could and just managed to scramble onto the muddy bank.

As soon as he got his breath back, he waddled to the middle of the island where just one small tree was growing. It was a tiny island but it looked big to Dippy. "No-one else is living on this island, so I shall claim it for my own," he said. "From now on it will be called *Duckling Island*."

He felt very pleased with himself, but all that swimming had made him very tired. So he sat in the sun and closed his eyes. The next minute he heard a loud flapping of wings and a big splashing sound. Opening his eyes he saw a swan had landed on the water.

"Get off the island," said the swan. "I'm going to build a nest here."

"You can't. This is *my* island," said Dippy, putting his beak in the air.

The swan came out of the river, threw out his chest and stretched his wings until he looked enormous. "*Whose* island is this?" he asked.

"M...m...mine," gulped Dippy, in a very small voice.

Just then Mrs Swan swam along. "This place is no good for a nest," she sniffed. "I shall need lots of bulrushes to hide it. There's a much better place further down the river."

So the swans swam off, leaving Dippy on his island.

Dippy put his beak in the air, puffed out his chest and spread his wings, just as the swan had done. "This is *my* island," he said, looking round proudly.

Then ripples appeared on the water and an otter popped out his head.

"Go away," said Dippy, who was really rather frightened. "This is my island."

The otter took no notice. He climbed out of the water and shook the wet drops off his sleek coat. "I'm looking for something to eat," he said.

He was licking his lips and watching Dippy in a very hungry way when he caught sight of a boat coming up the river. Quick as a flash, the otter dived back into the river.

"I'm glad he's gone," said Dippy, feeling much braver. "This is *my* island and I don't want anyone else on it." Then he turned round and saw the boat coming.

It was a large speed boat and it came roaring up the river, making big waves in the water. As it rushed by a huge wave washed right over the island, taking Dippy with it. "Help!" he spluttered.

By the time Dippy had got his breath back, Duckling Island was almost out of sight. The water was pulling him along so fast he could only just keep bobbing along.

He rushed along, faster and faster, and he closed his eyes, wondering what would happen to him. Suddenly, he felt himself being scooped into the air.

He opened his eyes and saw that he was dangling above the water in a big fishing net. "So you're in trouble again, Dippy," said a voice he knew.

"It's lucky I came fishing today," said Farmer Brown, as he lifted Dippy out of the net and put the little duckling in his coat pocket. "I'd better take you back where you belong."

Dippy peeped out of Farmer Brown's pocket and saw they were going along the river bank, past the stream and all the way back to the pond.

Then Farmer Brown lifted Dippy out of his pocket and put him on the pond where Mother Duck was waiting with all his brothers and sisters.

"Where *have* you been?" asked Mother Duck.

"I've been to see the river," said Dippy.

"What did you do there?" asked the frog, who had hopped over to see what the fuss was all about.

"I captured an island and then I named it Duckling Island. After that I had to fight everyone else who tried to get on it," said Dippy. "First I frightened off a swan, then I chased an otter away."

"You *did*?" gasped the frog, in surprise.

"After that, I got carried away by a big wave, and if Farmer Brown hadn't caught me in his fishing net, I expect I'd have had a lot more adventures," said Dippy, puffing up his chest, spreading his wings and putting his beak in the air.

Everyone thought Dippy was very brave and clever. But he didn't tell anyone what a lucky escape he'd had, and he has *never* been to Duckling Island again.

Frost Pictures

In winter, jumping from my bed
To part my curtains, blue and red,
I see upon the windowpane
A frosty fairyland again;

As though a secret, magic hand
Had painted there a wonderland
Of frozen ferns and castles tall,
And sparkling flowers, large and small.

But when the sun begins to rise
With beams so dazzling to my eyes,
The magic pictures quickly pass
And leave just water on the glass.

Simon's Special Snowman

Simon was looking out of the window and feeling very fed up. "I haven't got anything to do," he grumbled, "and there's nobody to play with in this street."

"Look, it's starting to snow," said his mother. "When it's deep enough you can go outside and make a snowman."

Simon watched the snow falling faster and faster. It got deeper and deeper, until Simon shouted: "There's plenty of snow to make a snowman. Hooray!"

Simon's mother helped him put on his coat and boots, then grabbing his warm gloves, he ran outside to play in the snow.

First he piled up the snow with a spade, to make the snowman's body,

then he rolled a great big snowball for his head. "How can I make his face?" he shouted to his mother, who was watching through the window.

In a few minutes she came out with two bottle tops for his eyes, a carrot for his nose and a piece of orange peel cut in a half-circle for his mouth. "What are you going to call him?" she asked.

"I'll call him Smiley Snowman," said Simon, "because he looks so happy."

Then Simon went indoors to have his tea and Smiley Snowman stayed outside. It began to get dark and all the street lights came on. "I wish I'd got someone to talk to," said Smiley, "but I can't see another snowman anywhere along this street."

Before Simon went to bed he took a last peep out of his bedroom window and said: "There's Smiley Snowman. I'll play with him again tomorrow."

But when Simon had gone to sleep, Smiley Snowman said: "I'm tired of staying out here all on my own. I'll go along the street and see if I can find someone to play with."

Smiley went down the garden path, opened the gate and began to move along the street with a funny, shuffling walk. But not one other snowman could he find, because Simon was the only boy in the whole street and the grown-ups hadn't made any snowmen to play with.

Smiley shuffled on through the town. By this time everybody else had gone to bed , so there was no-one to stop him.

At last Smiley reached the children's playground. He stopped and listened. He could hear a funny, squeaking noise. It was coming from one

of the swings.

There, at last, was another snowman! He was swinging to and fro, all on his own, looking very sad. But when he saw Smiley, he started to smile back. He jumped off the swing and called: "Do come and play on the see-saw!"

The other snowman's name was Toby Topper, because he was wearing an old top hat. He and Smiley had a lot of fun together in the playground. First they see-sawed up and down, then they whirled round and round on the roundabout. Then they tried the big slide.

"Whee, this is fun!" laughed Smiley. "I'm going to do that again."

Very soon they both started to feel very warm. As snowmen don't like to get hot, they found some long icicles and licked them like iced lollies.

"It is fun to have someone to play with," said Toby Topper. "I don't like being left here all by myself."

"Come home with me," said Smiley. "I'm sure Simon won't mind."

By the time they got back to Simon's garden the sun was just beginning to rise. Simon woke up and looked out of his window and saw *two* snowmen there. He couldn't believe his eyes.

He called his mother to come and see them, and she was very surprised. "I wonder how ever the other snowman go there?" she cried.

Then, after breakfast, some boys and girls came knocking at the door. "Can we have our snowman back?" they said. "We made him in the playground yesterday. We know he's our snowman because he's wearing a top hat, but we don't know how he got into your garden!"

They tried to move Toby Topper but he just would not budge. "It's no good, you'll have to stay and play with him in my garden," said Simon, by

now getting quite excited.

So they all played with Smiley and Toby Topper until the sun grew so warm, both snowmen began to feel very uncomfortable.

Then Simon's mother called everyone else indoors to have some orange juice and biscuits.

Smiley looked at Toby and Toby looked at Smiley. "I think it's time we went off to Snowmanland," they both said.

When Simon and his friends came back into the garden, Smiley and Toby Topper had disappeared. All they left behind was an old top hat lying on the ground.

Nobody found out where the snowmen had gone, but after that Simon always had lots of friends to play with.